T0145276

The Adventures of Lucas the Ant

LOST IN A STRANGE PLACE

BY

LEROY NABAUNS

ILLUSTRATIONS BY

EULA SAMUWEL

The Adventures of Lucas the Ant
LOST IN A STRANGE PLACE

iUniverse books may be ordered through booksellers or by contacting:

iUniverse
1663 Liberty Drive
Bloomington, IN 47403
www.iuniverse.com
1-800-Authors (1-800-288-4677)

Because of the dynamic nature of the Internet, any web addresses or links contained in this book may have changed since publication and may no longer be valid. The views expressed in this work are solely those of the author and do not necessarily reflect the views of the publisher, and the publisher hereby disclaims any responsibility for them.

Any people depicted in stock imagery provided by Getty Images are models, and such images are being used for illustrative purposes only.
Certain stock imagery © Getty Images.

ISBN: 978-1-5320-4231-7 (sc)
ISBN: 978-1-5320-4232-4 (e)

Library of Congress Control Number: 2018902215

Print information available on the last page.

iUniverse rev. date: 03/06/2018

Dedicated to...

My wife, that I love so

dearly. Also my

Friends

and family, who

waited for the

development of this

book.

Once upon a time their was an ant, the ant was named Lucas. Now Lucas was a very hard worker he was busy in the ant pile doing all his chores.

You see Lucas mother was the queen, and

her name was Queen Anne,

the highest and most loved Queen in all the

south. The Queen loved her

son Lucas.

Later that afternoon he met with his two friends Leo and Mike.

His friend mike said, "It's been a long day how about having some fun a little while", Mike said, "How about hide and seek. "

Lucas, "Okay just for a little while.

They ran in and out of the ant pile and found Lucas all the time. So Lucas had and idea, and went under the street curb. He said, ha, ha, they can't find me now. After a while he knew his friends couldn't find him. He started going back to the ant pile. His friends Leo and Mike noticed him coming and Leo yelled, "Hey Lucas, where were you?" Then mike yelled, "Hey Lucas look out!"

Just then, a blast of water and air blowing from under a big street sweeper passed by, and the water splashed against Lucas. He was trapped in water and he went floating down the street. Leo yelled, "Lucas!" The water wouldn't stop as it made its way to a drain, and it pulled Lucas in the drain. Lucas yells, "Whoa.....get me out of here! Mike hollers, "Lucas!!!"

The water turned him to the left and then to the right, and he began to float. The water finally stopped. Lucas was okay but where was he in this dark smelly place that barely had light. So he Lucas shouted out, "Help me, can anybody hear me!"

Then he looked and he could see a light from a water drain, and there was no water coming out.

So he crawled up the wall and through the drain. When he reached the street their was a lot of car horns blowing and people walking, as he dodged their feet.

So he started moving through some grass,

he found a park. All Lucas wanted

to do was take

a bath from that smelly sewer. Lucas found a beautiful

pond, took a piece of a sweet smelling leaf, and began

to wash himself.

All of a sudden the water started getting lower and lower. Then look like a big bubble started coming up. Some big eyes stared at him and a big red tongue followed, and there staring at him was a big frog that made deep base sounds like

("croaker, croaker") .

Lucas terrified whispered, "Oh
no my mother will never find me now." "Then he
asked the frog are,...are, you going to eat me?"
The frog said, "Eat you, a tiny little fellow like you
couldn't possibly fill me up." "No sir I like small
fish myself."

Lucas, "I didn't know but that's a good thing though." Frog, "Why are you here all by yourself anyway. There's always plenty of you guy's running around. Lucas, held his head down with a sad face and said, "Because I'm lost.

All of a sudden a grasshopper came along hopping up and down. He repeated every last thing he heard over and over. Grasshopper, "lost, lost, what is lost? The The frog said, "You don't know what lost is, he can't find his way home. The grasshopper said, "Home, home, home." "The frog said, yes home, you know where your family is."

Lucas, "No wait let me talk to him, you see maybe he's out here all on his own."

Frog, "huh he seem like a nut to me."

Lucas goes over to the grasshopper.

Grasshopper say's, "nut to me, nut to me, nut to me."

Lucas, "Stop that, wait, wait, and then he yells freeze!"

The grasshopper stood in one spot and started shaking all his legs was shaking, his body and head was shaking, and making some kind of sound. Grasshopper," Girrr, girrr, girrr. Lucas, "Are you breathing, I didn't say stop breathing. I said freeze, now breathe, breathe!" "You have to breathe to live." The grasshopper began breathing and catching his breath going, "Ah, ah."

The frog held his mouth tightly together with a smile on his face, but then he couldn't hold it anymore. He burst out laughing and rolled on the ground laughing harder and harder. Lucas fell to the ground laughing also. "The frog said, "He's funny."

The grasshopper came over to them and said, "He's funny ha, ha, ha." "He's funny ha, ha, ha."

Frog, "So, little ant what way did you come from?"

Lucas thought about it a second and said,

"Well my mother is queen of the south, hey south;

why didn't I think about that.

The frog and the grasshopper looked at

each other and said at the same time, "Queen!"

Frog, "So that make you a prince."

Lucas, "I don't look at it that way."

Frog, "Yes your highness I will to get you home, but there is one problem, a mean coyote named Bondua rules the south side of the park, and nobody gets in or out without asking him." "Lucas, "You know guys my mother always told me that the will is the way."

The frog stretched out his hand, Lucas put his hand on, the frog hand, and the grasshopper put his hand on, over and over as he jumped up and down. Lucas, "Now that we're all friends, frog I would like to call you Croaker, and grasshopper I would like to call you hopper, let's go."

Frog, "Uh your highness there is no way you can crawl there, do me the honor of getting on my back; and hold on." As they moved through the park all they could hear was all kinds of squeaking and chirping sounds from other animals.

Lucas, "Come on guys let's make this a happy park with a little song, give me some base croaks Croaker, and hopper you repeat after me."

♪ "My mother would always say,

That the will; is the way."

"No matter what nobody say;

"You can do it anyway,

"I may have lost my way;

But I'm not here to stay."

Because the will; is the way." ♪

The other animals in park danced to the tune, birds were singing more, and did their daily work better. But then trouble came, Bondua walked up to them and said, "Give me your riches prince."

Lucas noticed a piece of glass on the ground. Lucas whispers to Croaker, "You see that piece of glass down there, flash it in his face." Croaker raises the glass into the bright sunlight and the flashing and flickering became brighter and brighter and Bondua yelled, "Stop it, stop it! Lucas yells, "Freeze! and Hopper yells" "Girr...girr.." Bondua temporarily blinded by the light and scared by the sound runs way. Lucas yells to hopper, "Breathe."

As Lucas was leaving the park, he couldn't help but look back at all the insects and animals and smile. Lucas, "Hey that's the drain I went down, it want be long now." He came down from croaker and stood a couple of feet from the pile. Lucas yelled, "The will is the way!" The Queen had workers all around her, she said "Wait", wait a minute did you here that."

Lucas yelled louder, "The will is the way! The queen said oh god my baby is alive, she screamed," "Lucas! Lucas came closer to the pile and his friend Leo yelled it's "Lucas, "I thought I had lost you." They grabbed each other tight, and mike came hug him also. Then the queen came outside and everyone mumbled because she never comes out.

Lucas kneeled, looked up her and said, "You were right mom the will is the way and I fought all this way to come back to you.

Queen, "Get up my son" she hugged him tight and said, "I love so much." All the ants cheered. Lucas said, and this is my friends Croaker and hopper they helped me all the way." The queen said, "You're welcome here." The ants cheered more.

Hopper, "Welcome here, welcome here, welcome here." Croaker just looked on with a big old grin.

THE END

Printed in the United States
By Bookmasters